THE
HUNGER

THE HUNGER

ELAINE C. MARKOWICZ

authorHOUSE®

AuthorHouse™
1663 Liberty Drive
Bloomington, IN 47403
www.authorhouse.com
Phone: 1-800-839-8640

Published by AuthorHouse   09/07/2012

ISBN: 978-1-4772-6889-6 (sc)
ISBN: 978-1-4772-6890-2 (e)

Library of Congress Control Number: 2012916771

Any people depicted in stock imagery provided by Thinkstock are models,
and such images are being used for illustrative purposes only.
Certain stock imagery © Thinkstock.

This book is printed on acid-free paper.

Because of the dynamic nature of the Internet, any web addresses or links
contained in this book may have changed since publication and may no longer be
valid. The views expressed in this work are solely those of the author and do not
necessarily reflect the views of the publisher, and the publisher hereby disclaims
any responsibility for them.

For Billy

Prologue

There is a hunger in vampires that needs to be satiated: that for blood and that for sex. This desire becomes especially strong when a vampire senses his true love. Then nothing will satisfy him until he has her. It's his driving force.

Draegon Branson was such a vampire. When accidentally awakened by a young man seeking to rob his tomb, Draegon rose and satisfied his blood lust, turning the young man into his slave but had yet to satisfy his lust. He sensed her; alive, living in London, his true love, his bride; and he would search all of London to find her.

London, 1897

Chapter One

She stood on the corner in the drizzling rain waiting for the landlord to show her the apartment. Her grandmother, who raised her from a child, had recently passed away. Laurel couldn't afford the upkeep or rent on her grandmother's house and was forced to move to a cheaper residence. She found that residence in the paper. It wasn't in the best of London neighborhoods but it was what was best for her. She posted a letter to the landlord and he quickly responded. Now she wished he was as prompt. She was cold and damp from the sheet of drizzling rain pattering on her umbrella. She was about to change her mind and go home when a squirrely young man turned the corner fumbling with a ring of keys. He bobbed his head at her and sprint up an outer staircase. Laurel followed.

The door opened on a fair-sized landing. Directly before them was another, shorter stairway leading to another apartment. Laurel's was to their right. The young man unlocked her door and stood aside for her to enter. It was a moderate sized room, already furnished. The kitchen was but a few appliances in a catty-corner: an ice box, wood burning stove and a sink with hot and cold running water. The parlor contained a sofa, arm chair, low table, two lamp stands with oil lamps, a wardrobe, desk and chair. The kitchen had a small brown kitchen set. The only other room was the bathroom.

She turned to the young man fidgeting with the keys, waiting for her response. Laurel told him she wanted it and handed him the first month's rent. Taking her money, he turned and departed, leaving Laurel to look about the apartment one last time. She checked the fob pinned to her white front-pleated blouse. There was enough time for her to catch the train back to Grosvenor Square. With a lingering, farewell look, Laurel exited the apartment.

* * *

The rains broke through the sky just as Laurel got home. Changing out of her wet clothes into a night rail, she fixed herself dinner and after the dishes were cleared away she made a cup of tea. She lifted her eyes to the window over the sink; at the ribbons of lightning in the night. Tonight would be a good night for her to write her next mystery novel for the London Times newspaper. Besides the moderate inheritance and monies from the sale of the house, writing was her main source of income; as she sold her short stories to the paper.

She crossed the parlor when lightning bathed the room in blue. She gasped at the face pressed against the window and dropped her cup of tea. It shattered on the hardwood floor. When the lightning struck a second time, the face was gone. She stooped to pick up the broken pieces of the cup when the door burst open and a man, drenched to the bone, stormed into the parlor. He was a large man with shoulder-length black hair and glowing blue eyes. Fangs distended over his bottom lip when he growled.

Laurel slowly stood, staring at the frightening creature now dripping water on the floor. She started to back away, wondering where she could run that he wouldn't catch her. She doubted her locked bedroom door would deter him.

He beckoned a finger. She shook her head, walking backwards. Before he had the chance to turn and run he was on her. He swept her into his embrace, hungrily devouring her mouth. The points of his fangs pricked her lower lip and the sweet taste of her blood aroused him further. He picked her up and tossed her on the sofa. Laurel felt paralyzed by his eyes that kept her from screaming. He pulled off his shirt and climbed on top of her, pulling down the shoulders of her gown until her breasts were exposed to his gaze. He suckled on a nipple while his hand slid down her hip, over to the moist spot between her legs. He tickled the nubbin gaining pleasure in her reaction. Shamefully, her body involuntarily responded to his intimate touch. He had no patience with the fact she might be a virgin and thrust his phallus deep inside of her. Laurel arched her hips and cried out in pain and ecstasy. The creature continued to pump

3

inside of her; she undulating beneath him. At the moment of climax, he growled and sunk his fangs into her pulsating vein. She moaned with pain and pleasure as he suckled her sweet tasting blood. He had to force himself to stop before he drained her. As he moved away, Laurel passed out.

Laurel woke to the loud thunder clap with a gasp. She sat up and looked, disoriented, around the room. The sound of the rain and wind beating against the windows and the fire crackling in the fireplace was all that filled the quiet void. *What happened?* She wondered. She noticed the broken cup, the floor stained with tea. She must have passed out, falling onto the sofa seconds before she went unconscious. Laurel would never just lie down and nap after breaking a tea cup. She scrubbed the sleep from her face and stood; a bit woozy. Grabbing the arm of the sofa, she steadied herself and went on to clean up the mess.

Chapter Two

Laurel took a cabbie to her new apartment in the East End of London. The driver staid the team of horses and hopped down to open the door for the lady. He went took her luggage from the top of the carriage. Following her; the driver carried the heavy suitcases up the outer stairs, through her apartment door. She paid and tipped him for his services. He tipped his hat and quit the apartment, leaving the door opened. Laurel turned to close it when a young woman appeared in the doorway. Startled, she hitched her breath.

The girl quietly observed the room; lifting brown eyes on Laurel. "This used to be Cindy's room. The furniture is hers."

"Oh?" This gave Laurel reason to pause. If the girl returned for her furniture, she would be hard pressed to buy new furniture. "I'm Laurel." She introduced herself to the pretty blonde.

"She just upped and disappeared one day." The girl softly spoke.

"That's awful." Laurel empathized.

The girl nodded then turned and walked away. Laurel heard the soft patter of her feet on the stairs. As she reached the door, she saw the girl enter the upper apartment.

Chalking the girl up as strange, Laurel closed and locked the door.

*   *   *

She heard the slow, methodical footsteps on the outer stairs. Thinking it her upstairs neighbor, Laurel continued with her writing. That is, until she heard the doorknob jiggle. She turned from the desk and watched it move up and down. She held her breath, hoping the girl would go away. At least, she hoped it was the girl upstairs. After a long moment of tense silence, she heard the creak of the main door and the shuffle of feet on the stairs. Laurel got up and went to the window. She peeled aside the curtain and looked down on the street. Under the lamplight she saw a figure standing just by the perimeter of the light so he was cast in dark shadows. She quickly dropped the curtain, rechecked the lock on the door and went in the kitchen to make a cup of tea.

Chapter Three

After a fitful night's sleep, Laurel woke to start her day. She needed to go to market and purchase groceries and a few personal items. It would be a good way to get to know the neighborhood. So, dressing in a light green front pleated blouse and dark green bustle skirt, Laurel departed for her excursion.

At the market, Laurel bought produce, dry goods, and apples to bake a pie, ribbons for her chestnut hair, paper, quills and ink.

Coming home, hours later, she bumped into the squirrely young man. He was coming out of a room from under the stairs with a bag. He nodded to Laurel and kept walking.

Curiosity made her look into the room under the stairs. It was a laundry room. Laurel wondered why he never said anything about it. She hurried out of the room to question him about it but he was gone. With a sigh, she lugged her bags of food up the stairs.

The girl was coming down her stairs as Laurel entered the building. She nodded at Laurel. "Did you hear the news?" she asked Laurel.

"What news is that?"

"A girl was found dead near a pub here in the East End. Her throat was slashed. That's the third one this month.

Word has it the Ripper is back. He was never caught, you know."

"Yes, I do know." Laurel referred to the latter.

"Don't be walking about at nights. Or stay close to the lamplights and crowded streets." The girl warned.

"Thank you, you too."

The girl nodded. "I have to go out nights. I work in the pub where the killing took place."

"Can't you walk to and from work with someone?"

"I have someone who walks with me to work. I come home in the daylight, so it doesn't matter."

"I'm sorry but you never told me your name."

"Sherry." She replied and walked past Laurel out the door.

Laurel opened the door to her apartment and went inside, being sure to lock it. She thought to ask the landlord for a double lock. The news about the girl being killed so close to where she lived unnerved Laurel. Perhaps living here in the East End wasn't worth the few pence she paid.

*　　*　　*

She cooked the fish, she brought from the market, for dinner. Afterwards, with the dishes clean, she decided to make the apple pie. She mixed the ingredients for the dough and was rolling it out when the hairs on the back of her neck stood on end. Someone was in the room with her. She sharply turned and cried out. Draegon snarled with a wicked smile, took her in his arms and kissed her passionately. She, in turn, responded to his tongue tasting the caverns of her mouth. Moaning, she leaned in against him. He growled and spun her about, bending her over the table. He hiked up her skirts, teased her nubbin with his fingers, bringing wetness to her vagina. Draegon then thrust his cock up inside her. Laurel clung to the edges of the table as he pumped her hard and fast, until at the moment of their climax he bit into the vein in her neck. She gasped and fell unconscious. He laid her on the floor and departed.

Laurel woke, finding herself on the kitchen floor, her face sprinkled in flour, flour spilled on the floor around her and apples spilled and scattered. *Not again!* She bemoaned. *What was wrong with her that she kept passing out with no memory of what happened?* She slowly pulled herself up by a chair and sat down while the room slightly swayed. *Was she coming down with something?* Her black outs were starting to worry her. After a few minutes, she recouped and cleaned up the mess, finishing the pie.

Chapter Four

Laurel took her laundry downstairs and put a small load into the ringer washer. She noticed a newspaper on the table in the room and was about to start reading it when Sherry entered.

"Is this your paper?" Laurel inquired, holding it up.

"It was. You can read it."

"Thank you."

Sherry put the basket of her clothes on the table and looked at the occupied washer and then Laurel. She looked up from the paper and looked back at the washer.

"I'm sorry. I didn't know you wanted to use the washer today."

"It's okay. I'll just leave them here and you can put them in for me. Let me know when you did." Sherry suggested and departed.

Laurel wearily sighed. The girl was starting to tax her nerves.

Laurel hung her clothes on the line on the back of the property. She looked up at the building; feeling someone watching her. She saw a curtain move. It was her landlord. She was starting to wonder if he and Sherry were related; they were both strange and made her uncomfortable.

When she returned to the laundry room to fetch the newspaper she hadn't read, other than the headlines; the paper was gone. She only guessed that Sherry decided to take it back. Laurel shrugged. No matter, it was gruesome news about the women who had their throats slashed. The killer was still at large and people were beginning to fear the Ripper had returned for a second wave of serial killings.

*   *   *

Robert waited as the lid to the coffin opened. He dreaded the nights. He would always regret that night he broke the chain on the coffin in the hopes of finding jewelry; instead he found a living corpse that held him by the throat as he bit deeply into his vein, satisfying his first lust. Since then Robert has been Draegon Branson's obedient servant.

Draegon rose from his coffin and salaciously smiled at Robert who, despite being his servant in all ways, cringed when the vampire touched him. As he suckled his blood, his hand reached inside Robert's pants and fondled his cock, bringing it to an engorged erection. Draegon found that blood tasted better when he got the host aroused. Robert moaned, leaning back into Draegon's arms. When he climaxed, he nearly fainted. Draegon patted his servant on his flushed cheek.

"Well done." He complimented; as he did every night. "Now, go prepare my drink." He ordered.

Robert straightened his waistcoat and vest and hurried up the basement stairs.

Robert was in the parlor fixing Draegon's brandy when the vampire entered the kitchen from the basement stairs. He saw the newspaper on the table with the headlines about the killings.

"Robert!"

The squirrely young man hurried into the kitchen with his master's drink. "Sir?"

Draegon held up the newspaper. "What's this?"

"Uh, a newspaper?"

Draegon slapped him across the head with it. "What's it doing in my house?"

"I put it there, Sir. I meant to throw it away before you woke, I just forgot."

"Why did you have it in the first place?"

"I took it from the laundry room. I didn't think you'd want Miss Tuttle to see it."

"I don't want to see it either. You know I hate this trash." He slapped the paper. "They can't even get their details straight. I didn't slash their throats; I tore them open with my fangs when I tore their flesh." He shoved the paper at Robert. "Get rid of it."

"Yes, Sir."

"How is Miss Tuttle settling in?" he queried.

"Fine, Sir."

"Good. I have plans for her." He maliciously grinned. He picked up his glass of brandy and went in the parlor to sit in his favorite arm chair and savor his drink in front of the fireplace. Draegon didn't need the drink or fire for warmth; it was just one of the quirks he brought over when he turned.

Chapter Five

*I*t was dusk when Laurel came home from shopping. A man in black cloak and hat stood on the corner. Drawing closer to him, he tipped his hat and inclined his head. "Good evening." He greeted.

The fact he was so good looking made Laurel smile back. "Good evening."

"Would you like some help with those bags?"

"I only live across the street."

"Still, a lady shouldn't carry so many packages up the steps. Here, let me take a few." He took the packages before she could refuse.

They walked across the street and up the stairs. Laurel opened the door and turned to take the bags from the stranger. It just wouldn't look proper for a young man to enter a young lady's apartment. "Thank you, Sir. I can handle the rest from here." She assured and rushed inside before he could say another word.

Draegon stood on the steps with a malevolent smile.

* * *

The green mist slithered under the bedroom door, across the floor and hovered over Laurel in her sleep. She gasped like a resuscitating victim from the pressure on her body. The mist took the shape of a man. His glowing eyes deeply peered Laurel's green ones as he cupped her breast. Laurel moaned, slowly undulating beneath him. He bowed his head to suckle on the nipple freeing his hand to enter his fingers into the moist folds between her legs. Laurel wrapped her arms around his neck, tilting her head and rolling her eyes, accompanied by soft moans. He slowly removed his fingers and replaced them with a hard thrust of his shaft. Laurel gasped, thrusting her hips upward.

Draegon rode her hard and fast, enjoying the pleasure he gave her and he received in return. Her fingernails dug into the flesh of his back, drawing blood. The scent sent him careening into an insatiable drive. He could hold back no longer and reached around to sink his fangs into her pulsating vein. Laurel cried out and fell limp when he spilled his seed inside her and suckled her blood. She fell back into a deep sleep. He kissed her softly parted lips and stroked her damp, chestnut hair. "Sleep well, my beloved." He said in hushed tone and departed.

* * *

Robert met Colin at the pub where Sherry worked. She served them once or twice but asked no questions. She went about her business. Robert took Colin to the phaeton in the back alley to do his business. He leaned over Colin, covering his mouth with his own. His hand slid inside Colin's shirt, rubbing his nipples. His other hand slid into his trousers, fondling the engorged penis. The two were oblivious to their surroundings until suddenly someone snatched Colin, throwing him out of the phaeton and against the wall. His fangs sunk into the young man's neck and Robert cried out.

"No! Stop!"

Draegon ignored him, sucking on Colin's tangy blood as he continued to manipulate his cock. After draining his blood, Draegon snapped his neck. The man's body fell to the ground in a heap. Robert jumped out of the phaeton and stooped beside his lover. He lifted angry eyes on Draegon.

"Can't you leave me one lover?"

Draegon shrugged and vanished.

*   *   *

Laurel answered the door on the squirrely young man she believed to be her landlord Mr. Branson. "Is there something wrong?" she queried.

"Mr. Branson would like the pleasure of your company for dinner tonight." He informed with what sounded like regret.

"Mr. Branson? Oh, I thought you were him."

Robert shook his blonde head. "No, I'm Mr. Hayes, his assistant."

Laurel got the impression, from his tone of voice if she said 'no', Mr. Hayes would suffer the consequences. So, she agreed.

Robert tremulously smiled. "Dinner will be served at eight."

"Tell Mr. Branson thank you for the invite and I'll be there promptly at eight o'clock."

Robert inclined his head, turned and departed.

*   *   *

Laurel knocked on Branson's door. Robert answered. "Miss Tuttle, do come in."

Dressed in a blue bustle skirt with matching short jacket and a lighter blue ruffle front blouse, Laurel nervously entered. She wondered why the landlord would invite her to dinner. Did he do this for Sherry as well when she moved in?

Mr. Branson waited in the parlor, drink in hand. He slyly grinned when she halted, recognizing him as the stranger who helped carry her bags the other day.

"Ah, Miss Tuttle. Welcome to my humble abode."

"Mr. Branson. Thank you for inviting me."

He proffered a hand to the gold and white settee. "Do sit down. Robert will bring you a drink. Do you like brandy?"

"I don't imbibe."

"Well, tonight will be a first. Brandy for Miss Tuttle, Robert." He ordered.

"Yes Sir."

"Do you always invite new tenants to your house for supper, Mr. Branson?"

"I like to get to know my tenants on a more personal nature. Do you agree, Miss Tuttle?"

She accepted the glass of brandy from Robert. "It depends on how personal." She replied and cautiously sipped the drink. It burned going down but then relaxed warmth spread over her body.

"Do you like it?" Draegon asked.

"A bit strong for my taste, but surprisingly, yes."

"Robert, prepare the dining room." Branson ordered.

"Yes, Sir." Robert bowed and went into the dining room.

"I thought Mr. Hayes was supposedly you, Mr. Branson." She confessed, sipping more brandy.

"Tenants often make that mistake because they rarely see me in the beginning. Robert handles most of my transactions."

"Thank you again for helping me with my packages the other day."

"You're more than welcome."

"Why didn't you introduce yourself then?"

"I wanted to surprise you."

"You certainly did."

"It doesn't matter now. You've met me and now we know each other."

"Well, we're acquainted." She corrected, sipping the remainder of the brandy.

Draegon took the glass and stood, "Here, let me refill that." He went to the sideboard where the liquor was kept and poured her more brandy. A wicked smile touched his lips as he handed her the full glass.

She was everything he wanted in his bride. When first he made love to her, Draegon knew, without a doubt, she was the one he was destined for. She was the reincarnation of his former fiancée who died before they could marry. Even as his father chained him inside his coffin Draegon swore when he awoke he would find his woman.

Robert announced that dinner was served and the two stood. Draegon took Laurel's hand and led her into the dining room. He pulled out her chair and she sat down. "Robert, you can leave now. You can have the rest of the night off to do what *pleasures* you."

Robert bowed his head, said his 'good nights' and exited the house.

Draegon served the soup and sat down across from her at the small, rectangular table. "How's the soup?" he queried, anxious for her approval.

She took a few spoonfuls of the vegetable broth and nodded. "It's fine, thank you."

"Miss Tuttle, I have a proposition for you."

Laurel lowered the spoon and stared at him, hoping he wasn't implying what she thought. He laughed.

"Nothing sordid, I assure you."

Laurel relaxed.

"I understand you're a writer."

He must have read her stories in the paper to know that. "Yes, I write short mystery stories for the papers."

"How would you like to write my biography?"

"I don't know if I could."

"I'll give you all of the material you'll need."

"I suppose. It does sound like an interesting challenge."

"We would have to work closely. Does that bother you?"

She hesitated a moment. "I, uh . . ."

He held up a hand, "I assure you, I'll be the perfect gentleman."

Laurel studied his handsome face. She had a hard time denying this man anything. One look from those dark brown eyes and she was melted butter. "Very well, Mr. Branson, I'll do it."

"You won't regret it. Will this be your first book?"

"Yes."

He lifted his glass in a toast. "Then here's to your success."

"It will be *our* success since we'll be collaborating."

"If you insist on sharing credit, then I welcome it."

Laurel smiled and sipped her brandy.

*   *   *

Robert drove his phaeton to the pub. Tonight he was free to find a guy and have sex without interference from Draegon since he was occupied with Laurel. He did feel bad luring her into the dragon's den knowing what his master had in store for her but he couldn't worry about it; he needed to take care of his needs.

He sat in his usual booth and watched the male patrons sitting at the bar alone. For a while no one interested him until he caught the eyes of a fair haired young man watching him. Robert ordered the barmaid to bring the guy what he was drinking. He watched and waited. The young man soon sauntered over to Robert's table.

"Thank you for the drink."

"You're welcome." He extended his hand. "I'm Robert Hayes."

"Brad Thomson."

"Hello, Brad Thomson."

They sat and drank for a while before Brad suggested they go to his apartment. Robert drove them over to Brad's place where they didn't waste time stripping of their clothes and climbing into bed. Robert embraced Brad with a searing kiss and Brad responded. Their tongues danced in the cavern of Brad's mouth. Robert moved down to suck one of Brad's nipples while Brad rubbed Robert's with the pad of his thumb. Robert didn't waste time moving to Brad's engorged erection. Brad moaned with pleasure as Robert wrapped his lips around his head and suckled on it until Brad spilled his seed into his mouth. Robert rolled onto his back taking Brad with him and eased Brad's anus onto his spear. Together they rocked until Robert released himself into Brad. Both fell limp, panting and in a sweat. Both were satiated. It was nice to make love with a guy without worrying about Draegon appearing to ruin his night.

*   *   *

After four brandies Laurel was pliable and ready for Draegon. He carried her upstairs to the main bedroom. He removed his cravat, waistcoat and shirt before climbing onto the bed beside Laurel who watched with dreamy eyes. His body was an artist's sculpture. She should stop what was about to happen but didn't have the energy. Besides, she was more than curious about the pleasure he could bring her.

Draegon undid her jacket, removed it and her blouse. His fingers slid the straps of her chemise from her shoulders, exposing her rosy nipples. He lowered his head and suckled one of them while he kneaded the other with his hand. Laurel groaned with pleasure, unable to fight him if she wanted to. She pushed her breasts upward to get the fullness of his mouth around them. He pulled off her skirt and chemise. His kisses trailed down her stomach to the chestnut bush between her thighs and taunted the folds with his tongue. Laurel cried out, thrusting her hips to get more. Draegon softly laughed at her demands. Her legs fell apart; she grabbed onto his silky black hair that hung to her shoulders and tugged at it, pulling his head forward. She wanted more and she wasn't ashamed to ask for it.

He rolled onto his back, taking her with him and sat her on his cock. She gasped, thrusting back her head and rolling her eyes. He took hold of her hips and rocked her back and forth until she picked up the rhythm and rode him like a stallion. He moaned with great pleasure trying to make it last until he felt he would explode and shot his seed within her. She fell limp in his arms, laying her head on his lightly furred chest. Her damp skin slid on his cold, slick body and she wondered why she didn't hear or feel a heartbeat.

Draegon held her in his arms as she peacefully drifted off to sleep.

Chapter Six

*L*aurel woke in a stupor. She glimpsed the clock on the mantle. It was after ten o'clock. Someone was knocking on the door. Thinking it was Draegon, she pulled herself off of the sofa, wrapping a robe about her night rail and answered the door. It was Robert, holding a stack of papers and a small, black, leather bound book.

"Mr. Branson asked me to bring these up to you so you could get started making notes for his book."

"Is he sleeping in late as well?" she queried.

"Uh, no, he's already out and about. He doesn't come home until evening. He may want to see you then."

"Very well."

Robert tipped his hat, bowed at the waist and hurried out of the small hallway.

Laurel shrugged, glancing at the papers and book in her hand as she closed the door. She started to read the first page. He was born April, 1600. But that couldn't be. That would make him near two-hundred. It must be his grandfather, for Draegon didn't look a day over twenty and five. She put the papers on the kitchen table and proceeded to make coffee to wake her up. She was still bothered by the sensual dream she had about her landlord. Her face flushed and she felt warm and moist below thinking about it. Surely he wasn't interested in her that way. She shook her head.

She had to stop thinking of *him that way*. It could only lead to trouble.

*   *   *

After doing a small load of clothes and hanging them out to dry in the back yard, Laurel spent the afternoon reading the notes Robert dropped off. His mother talked about what a sweet young man Draegon was but then when he turned twenty and five he began to change so much that it frightened her. His fiancée killed herself on the wedding day, sending Draegon into a melancholy mood. He would disappear during the day and most of the night. The family saw less of him. Laurel empathized with Mr. Branson. But his age and the years of the journal didn't seem right. How could he be a young man in the mid-seventeenth century? Surely, there was a mistake.

Laurel got so caught up in the notes and journal that when she looked up at the clock it was already five o'clock in the P.M. and she still had her clothes hanging up outside. Leaving the papers on the kitchen table she hurried downstairs and around the back surprised to find Draegon Branson caressing Sherry. She felt disappointment; not that she should or feel jealous because he never made any indication she was nothing more than his tenant and collaborator on his book. She waited in the laundry room until she saw Sherry pass by and heard her footsteps on the outer stairs above her. She picked up the wicker basket and went out back to take down her clothes.

As she came around to the stairs she jumped seeing Mr. Branson standing at the bottom of them, smiling at her. "Mr. Branson." She coolly greeted.

He took the basket of clothes from her. "Allow me."

"Really, I could carry them."

"Then what sort of gentleman would I be?"

"Are you gentleman, Mr. Branson?"

"Have I treated you poorly, Miss Tuttle?"

She hesitated. "Not so far."

"And I won't."

They reached the top of the steps and Laurel unlocked the door. She went to take the basket but he held onto it. "I thought I may come in and discuss the notes I sent up earlier."

Laurel hesitated.

Draegon looked about. "Oh, don't worry about improprieties here in the East End, Miss Tuttle. Now, if you would open your door?"

She hesitantly did so and invited him into her apartment. He put the basket on the floor near the kitchen. He saw the papers on the table. "Did you get a chance to read any of it?"

"Yes. I'm sorry about your fiancée. She must have been in terrible pain to do such a thing."

"She took the coward's way out and killed herself so she wouldn't have to marry me." He bitterly replied.

"You can't know that and there's nothing cowardly about taking one's life. Like I said, she must have been in terrible pain."

"What else did you read?" he changed a subject too painful to talk about.

"That your mother thought you a sweet, young man."

"I told you, I'm a gentleman." He grinned and she smiled.

"But I'm confused by the years."

"My mother was distraught when she wrote that journal; she probably wrote the wrong year." He lied.

"Yes, I read how distraught she was after your fiancée died; you became sullen and hard to reach."

"It's true, and I have been sullen until I met you."

"What?"

He slyly grinned, "It's just that you're so pleasant to be around."

"Thank you." She hesitantly replied.

"I speak only the truth."

He was standing uncomfortably close to her. "Mr. Branson, I think you should leave."

His fingers bit into her arms. His lips came down on hers. Laurel struggled at first but relinquished to his persistence. His kiss trailed to the swell of her breast and with agile and swift fingers removed her blouse, leaving her exposed in her white chemise: two nipples strained against the material. His mouth bent to her breasts and alternately suckled them. She moaned; her head tilted. His eyes raked the firm breasts and peaked nipples before he swept her into his arms and carried her to the sofa. "Tonight, my dear, you're going to remember."

She didn't know what he meant and she didn't care; she shamelessly gave herself to him. She helped him remove the remainder of her clothing. Draegon stood back as he undressed. He smiled that she gawked at the large penis standing at attention. "You've never looked upon a man, Laurel?"

"No." she flushed, peeling her gaze way, embarrassed.

He slid beside her on the couch. His penis tapped her thigh and she gasped with a slight start. He caressed her cheek. "Relax, there's no need to be embarrassed or a shamed."

"I'm not." She said, looking deep into his dark brown eyes.

He pressed his open mouth on hers: their tongues danced in their passion. Draegon's hand slid down her hip to the moist sheath beneath the chestnut bush. Her legs fell open, welcoming his touch. Aware of what she was doing, Laurel felt or showed no shame in their lovemaking; she was young and curious. Draegon lifted himself to slide his phallus inside of her. Once in her, Draegon lost control and drove her hard and fast until his essence exploded. Laurel cried out and fell limp in his arms.

"Did you enjoy it, Laurel?" he gently asked, stroking her hair. It took all of his control not to bite her and suckle her blood. She wasn't ready to know the truth.

Her face flushed, suddenly uncomfortable being naked with him in the cold reality afterwards. Draegon surreptitiously smiled.

Laurel started to sit up. "We should start working on the book before I get too tired." She'd been feeling run down of late. She passed it off as a bug.

Draegon took her arm and pulled her down into his arms. "Relax. We have plenty of time to start the book. I'm not done with you yet." He huskily said and made love to her again and again until he could no longer control his hunger for blood and sunk his fangs into her neck. Laurel gasped, and then weakly laid her head on his cool chest and went to sleep. She would remember their love making but not his sucking her blood.

Chapter Seven

*T*he following morning, Laurel woke up late. She was naked and it took her a few moments to remember what happened. She quickly sat up. Bad mistake; the room started to spin. She laid her head on the back of the sofa. Her body ached and she felt weak. Is this how a woman is supposed to feel after sex? Her face flushed at the memories flashing through her head. She leaned forward burying her face in her hands. What had she done? She was ruined! Her reputation was scandalized. She felt like a cheap harlot. What was she to do? She had to stop working on Mr. Branson's book. She could not afford to be intimate with a man she barely knew.

She got up, slipping on her robe, and went in the kitchen to make coffee. The papers were still spread out on the table. After the coffee percolated Laurel sat down and went over the notes and journal; still perplexed by the years. Did he mean it when he said his mother got confused and got the years wrong? Could the woman have been that confused that she got all of the years wrong? Laurel guessed it had to be or that would have made Mr. Branson two-hundred years old.

And what about his fiancée? How long ago did she die and how? There seemed to be pieces of the puzzle of Draegon Branson missing. Laurel sipped her coffee and leaned back in the chair with a sigh. Draegon was now in her blood. There was no denying her deep attraction to the man with silky raven hair and molten chocolate eyes. His body was perfection. And his love making was thrilling. She pushed the papers aside. She would put them together to bring back to him later. For now she was going to get dressed and go to market. Shopping always cleared her head.

*　　*　　*

Robert woke in his lover's arms. With Draegon preoccupied with Miss Tuttle, Robert spent a good deal of time at Brad's apartment, sharing their lovemaking. Brad was an excellent lover. He knew how to bring Robert to completion. He laid thinking of their passion the night before and smiled. He started getting excited thinking of how Brad sucked his shaft and how he inserted it into Robert's buttocks. He studied Brad's face. He was handsome. He lightly caressed his golden blonde hair. He could see himself spending a lifetime with Brad.

Brad groaned and opened those beautiful green eyes. He smiled at Robert. His hand gently caressed Robert's blonde furred chest, watching with pleasure as Robert grew harder. He trailed his kisses from his nipples, down his soft belly to the blonde tuft around his penis. He licked the engorged head. Robert moaned, weaving his fingers in Brad's long hair. Robert pushed Brad's head down on his cock and groaned deep in his throat as Brad suckled hard on him, bringing Robert to release. Brad kissed Robert. He could taste himself on Brad's lips. He in turn, satisfied Brad. It was a great way to start the day. He didn't want to think about what his master would say when he arrived home to an empty house the night before, nor for the moment did he care.

*   *   *

Robert answered the door of his master's house. Laurel stood holding a packet of papers in her hands. "Is Mister Branson at home?"

"Let her in, Robert." Draegon ordered from somewhere behind Robert.

Robert threw open the door and Laurel entered; her fingers nervously fidgeting with the packet.

"I'm bringing these back to you. I can no longer, in good conscience, continue our endeavor."

"What do you mean?" he demanded.

She glimpsed Robert standing nearby. Draegon turned to his servant. "Leave us." He ordered.

Robert popped on his hat and hurried out the front door.

"I feel that after what happened I can no longer work closely with you. It wouldn't be proper."

He lifted his right eyebrow, "What happened?"

Her face flushed. "I'd rather not repeat it." She snipped

"Repeat what?"

"Stop it! I know what you're doing." She angrily thrust the packet at him. "I will also start looking for a new flat."

"That isn't necessary."

"I feel it is. It just isn't proper that we work together."

"Who has to know what we did?"

"I know and that's enough. I allowed you to ruin me for any other man."

He peered deep into her green eyes. "Good. I don't want to share you with any other man."

"Good night, Sir." She snipped and started to walk towards the door.

He watched her leave; a sly smirk on his face.

*   *   *

Robert sat in his favorite pub, sipping on his pint. The foul London weather didn't seem to stop the regular patrons from visiting. He watched the door and his face lit up seeing Brad enter. His friend closed his umbrella and made his way to Robert's table. Sherry brought them a second pint.

"You sure she won't say anything to your employer about me? I don't want to get you into trouble. You know how people frown on us because we're different."

"I assure you, she won't say anything to my employer." It wasn't their being different that concerned Robert but what Draegon would do to Brad when he discovered Robert had a lover.

They were chatting to the background of glasses clinking, laughing and thunder when the door opened and Robert paled. "Oh God, no." he cried in a low voice. "Quick, let's get out of here."

"What?"

"Now, we have to leave, my employer just walked in."

"Won't he think we're just two guys talking?"

"Trust me; he has a sixth sense about these things. Let's go."

Brad stood with Robert, leaving the tab on the table. "Where should we go?"

"Out the back door. Hurry!"

Brad ran behind his lover down a dim hallway and through the back door that opened onto the alley. "Where are we going?"

"Any place but here." Robert declared. "Did you bring your barouche?"

"I took a cab."

"I have my phaeton on the corner. Come on."

As they climbed into the vehicle Robert heard Draegon's voice in his head. "*Do you really think you can run from me, Robert?*"

He nearly crashed into a lamp post.

"Be careful." Brad chided. "Hell wasn't the place I planned going tonight."

Robert glimpsed Brad. He was so adorable and he would laugh if not for the seriousness of the situation.

Chapter Eight

When Robert came around the corner of the apartment building to collect the rent from Laurel and Sherry he saw the paper boy. He managed to catch a glimpse of the bold print on the paper the boy was waving. He stopped to buy it. Robert read the title story of a young man found brutally slain in his flat. His hands shook, tears filled his blue eyes. "No! No, it can't be him. It can't be Brad!" But as sure as he denied it, he was just as sure it *was* Brad. He dashed around the corner, hopped onto his phaeton and clicked the reins. The horses whinnied and galloped down the street.

As he arrived at Brad's apartment building police were circling it. He tried to get in but the detective stopped him. "That's a crime scene; you can't enter."

"I'm the victim's friend." He frantically informed, anxious to see Brad.

"He's already been taken to the morgue. What's your name, Sir?"

"It doesn't matter." He retorted and climbed back onto the phaeton. Clicking the reins, he took off.

Robert shortly returned home and went down the basement. He pounded on the coffin lid, crying. "You killed him! You son of a bitch, you killed him!" He slid down on his knees and pressed his face against the coffin. "You killed him. Oh Brad, I'm so sorry."

He saw the spike lying on the floor and slowly picked it up. His hand shook as he opened the coffin. Draegon lay in repose, oblivious to what Robert was about to do. Robert lifted the spike over his head and came down with a hard thrust but stopped short of Draegon's chest. His hands were shaking uncontrollably. He couldn't do it. He wasn't a monster like the creature that lay in the coffin. He slammed down the lid and fell upon it, crying.

*   *   *

Laurel answered the door. Robert stood on the other side. "Are you here for the rent?" she asked.

He nodded. She curiously noted his red rimmed eyes and splotchy face. Not wanting to pry, she went in the kitchen drawer and procured the monies necessary for the rent. She handed him the money and he counted it and put it in his pocket. He turned to go up the stairs when Sherry's door opened.

"Oh, Mr. Hayes, are you here for the rent?" she called down.

He nodded with a sniffle.

"Be right down." She closed the door and shortly popped back out and went downstairs.

Laurel closed her door.

"What's wrong, Mr. Hayes?" Sherry asked, handing him the money.

"Nothing." He sniffled, counting the pounds.

"You look like you've been crying." Sherry noted. She glimpsed Laurel's closed door. She looped arms with Robert. "Come, let's go outside."

They strolled down the outer steps. "What happened? What's gotten you so upset?"

He wanted to tell her what a monster her landlord was but couldn't: he feared the repercussions. Instead he said. "My friend was brutally murdered last night in his flat."

Sherry put a hand to her mouth. "Oh my, that was your friend I read about?"

Robert nodded. "He never did anything to anybody." He sniffed back the tears about to shed.

"I'm so sorry. Do you think it was the serial killer? But he kills outside; in alleys or by the Thames."

"What difference does it make?" he hotly retorted. "He's dead!" He didn't mean to be so callous but his grief was stronger than his manners. He walked away.

*　*　*

Robert stood in the basement, his body in a sweat, as the coffin lid opened. Draegon climbed out of his casket and approached Robert but he didn't drink his blood. Instead he wrapped his hand around his throat, lifting him off of his feet. Robert clung to the hand that was choking him.

"Did you think I wouldn't know you tried to kill me earlier, Robert?"

"You killed my lover. Why? Why can't you leave my men alone?"

Draegon pulled him closer. "Because I like the way your kind tastes: oh so sweet and naughty." He then tossed him across the room. Robert fell on a stack of boxes and tumbled to the floor with them.

He struggled to stand up, pushing the boxes away. By the time he stood Draegon was already gone.

*   *   *

Laurel went down to the backyard to collect her clothes that had been hanging on the line all day. As she unclipped them and put them in the basket she noticed Sherry and Draegon. He was kissing her neck. Sherry didn't seem to mind his blatant display of affection.

Draegon slowly turned his head and looked directly at Laurel. Never had she seen such a malevolent expression. She shook her head and quickly tossed the remaining clothes in the wicker basket and exited the backyard.

*   *   *

Laurel took a bath later that night. As she climbed from the tub to towel dry a green fog slithered, snake-like, under the apartment door. When she came out of the bathroom she paused, mesmerized by the fog that slowly took the shape of a frightening creature with long, pointed fangs and translucent eyes that seemed to glow. He snarled at Laurel. She was too transfixed to move. With a growl, Draegon snapped the towel from her naked body and swung her up into his arms, carrying her to the sofa.

Laurel was too frightened to struggle against him. He swiftly divested his clothing and slid on top of her, assaulting her lips with his own. His hand kneaded the soft flesh of her breasts; his thumb rubbed the rosy bud. Laurel moaned and slipped her arms around him, holding him tight against her. He was ice cold against her hot skin. Somehow the sensation excited her. His hand moved down her hip, over her thigh, until his fingers met with the hot moist vagina. It felt so good. His fingers stroked both the nubbin and the nib, causing Laurel to shriek with passion.

"More." She whispered, thrusting her hips to his touch, her body demanding it harder and faster.

Draegon was more than happy to comply. He gave her what her body demanded. His own breath was ragged. She was ready for him. He thrust his shaft into her moist sheath. Laurel gasped, her body thrusting upward, her head rolled back on the pillow. Together they rode the tide of passion until Draegon released his cold semen into her and fell limp atop of her. He clasped his hands on her flushed cheeks and looked into her hooded eyes.

"You can't deny me your body, Laurel; it belongs to me and only me, though you won't remember any of it. It isn't time." He kissed her full, red lips. "Until another night." He dressed as she watched him through transfixed eyes and saw him egress out the apartment door.

Chapter Nine

*L*aurel woke alone and naked beneath the covers on her couch. She sat up wondering why she would be this way. She woke like this once before when she gave herself to Draegon. But she didn't remember him being there last evening. She leaned her elbows on her lap and covered her face in her hands, shaking her head. *What was happening to her?* This wasn't the only time she couldn't remember what happened to her and found herself in a precarious position.

She rose to get dressed and make coffee when she heard someone outside her door. The sound was followed by a soft knock. Laurel wrapped a robe around her and cautiously opened the door a crack. No one was in the hall but a package lay at her feet. She stooped to pick it up, looked about and then closed the door. She noted the package in her hands. It was Mr. Branson's notes for his book; the book she said she wouldn't do. She wished she could move but she couldn't afford to at the moment which made living at her present residence with Draegon Branson as her landlord very uncomfortable.

*   *   *

Robert came into the pub and out of the rain. His mood was as gloomy as the weather. He sat in his favorite chair and waited for the barmaid to bring him a pint. He wanted to pour his sorrows into the beer. He missed Brad terribly. Was he to remain celibate for the rest of his life? Every man he became involved with died at the hands of his master Draegon Branson.

It was while thinking this that a young man approached his table and sat down beside him. "Weather has you down?" he asked.

Robert looked over at the man. He was very good looking; nothing close to Brad but he was pleasant to look at. "I lost my friend."

"I'm sorry to hear it. What happened?"

"He was murdered by London's serial killer."

"The one rumored to be Jack the Ripper returned?"

Robert nodded and gulped a few mouthfuls of his beer. He put the stein down and glanced at the young man. "I'm really sorry but I'm not in the mood to converse. I'd like to be left alone."

The man stood, holding up his hands. "Not a problem. And, again, I'm sorry for the loss of your friend."

Robert watched him walk away and join another guy at a distant table.

He sighed and drank his beer. *Damn you, Draegon, I should have driven that stake through your heart when I had the chance.* He bitterly thought. He checked his fob watch. It was past three o'clock. With this dark and dreary weather Draegon was likely to rise early. He wouldn't be there and he didn't care what his master thought or did to him. His life was miserable as long as Draegon was alive.

*   *   *

Laurel sat at her desk writing. It was the perfect weather for writing her latest horror novel.

"Laurel."

She screamed, dropping the pen that smeared ink on her paper. Holding her racing heart she turned and looked up at Draegon. "How did you get in here?"

"Through the door."

"It was locked."

"So you thought."

"I was sure."

"Well I'm here, so apparently not."

She took a few deep breaths to calm herself down. "Just don't ever sneak up on me." She irately scolded.

"I didn't sneak up on you; you just didn't hear me." He looked over her shoulder at the work she was doing. "Writing my book?"

"No. I told you I wasn't doing it. I'm not comfortable being alone with you. Now, please leave."

"You're not going to play the prudish maiden, are you?"

Her face flushed. "If you mean I feel a shamed of what I did, yes."

He caressed her check; so warm and soft. "There's nothing to be a shamed of, Laurel. You didn't do anything wrong."

"But we did. Intimacy is shared with a marriage partner."

"Are you asking me to marry you?"

Her face reddened with embarrassment and anger. "No! Now, please leave my flat. It doesn't look proper."

Draegon softly chuckled. "Worried about who might see me come in here?"

"Yes."

"I told you, this is the east end. You won't find many people in the ton here. And personally I don't care what anyone thinks."

"Obviously." She snipped. "Now, please go."

He took her hand and kissed it. "As you wish." His piercing eyes transfixed her. Slowly she rose to her feet. He took her in his arms and seared her lips with his. She slid her arms around his neck matching his fiery kisses.

He lifted her into his arms. "You can't dismiss me so easily, my beloved." He carried her to the sofa and laid her down. He climbed on top of her, continuing with his assaulting kisses. She clung to him, thrusting her body up against him, afraid if she let go he would disappear forever. This felt so right. His lips trailed to her cleavage. Laurel moaned as he rubbed her hardened nipple through the muslin material of her bodice. Draegon slowly untied it and lowered his head to suckle one of the rosy buds.

Laurel's breath came in shallow pants. Pants that turned into shrieks as his fingers found the moist slit beneath her skirts.

"Oh, Draegon!"

"Still want me to leave?" he taunted.

"No, no! Stay, take me into your arms and make love to me all night." She breathlessly begged.

He wickedly chuckled and hiking up her skirts, he pulled off her petticoat with one swift motion and thrust his penis into her hot sheath. Laurel cried out, throwing her pelvis upward, digging her nails into his back nearly tearing through his shirt. And just as they reached climax, his fangs descended and plunged into the softness of her neck. She rolled her eyes with a gasp and both fell limp on the sofa. He lay on top of her, stroking her raven hair. "I will make love to you all night, my sweet but you won't remember it. Not yet."

*   *   *

It was late when Robert stumbled home. The house was dark and he hoped Draegon was still out; though it was getting close to daybreak. So when Draegon spoke to him he nearly jumped out of his skin.

"Did you have a nice evening, Robert?"

He turned about as Draegon turned on the nearby lamp. He was seated in his favorite chair with a drink.

Robert pulled up his shoulders. "Yes, yes I did." He snipped.

"You weren't here when I woke up."

"I know. I went to the pub."

"To cry into your drink over your lost friend?" Draegon taunted.

"Brad, his name was Brad. You're a monster and I rue the day I opened your coffin."

Draegon was suddenly up and holding Robert by his throat. "You should have killed me, Robert."

"I should have." He retorted.

Draegon tightened his grip around Robert's throat. "Now I should kill you."

"Go ahead. I just don't care anymore."

Draegon squeezed Robert's throat, his fangs descended and his piercing eyes burrowed into Robert's eyes. Robert's face was turning purple. He relaxed, waiting mercifully for his death. Instead Draegon pushed him into the liquor cabinet. "Go to bed, Robert. I won't kill you tonight."

Robert climbed to his feet and stumbled up the stairs to his room. Draegon sat his chair and finished his drink in the dark.

Chapter Ten

She woke with bad chills and achy body. Laurel sat up wrapping the blanket around her. The fire in the hearth had gone down and the damp weather didn't help how she felt. She stood and threw another log on the fire, stoking it until it blazed. Laurel stood before it, shivering. She must have caught a bug. A hot bath might help chase the chills away.

The steamy water helped chase away the chills. She stretched out in the tub and, laying her head back, relaxed and closed her eyes.

Someone whispered her name, "Laurel. Laurel, soon you will be my bride and will join me in my eternal torment." Draegon stood before her with translucent eyes and a malevolent grin. He beckoned his hand. "Come to me, Laurel."

She moved towards him in a trance, taking his hand. He pulled her into his arms and kissed her. Laurel moaned, tilting her head, exposing her neck. And then he opened his mouth, revealing two pointed fangs . . .

Laurel sat up with a gasp, looking about the bathroom for Draegon. She splashed water on her face. The chills were returning. She quickly washed, rinsed, and got out of the tub to towel dry. Not feeling well and the weather being what it was, Laurel decided to spend the day indoors, writing, so she wore her heavy cotton nightdress, robe and slippers.

The room was warmer. The fire took the dampness from the air. Laurel put the kettle to boil for a cup of tea. She would make a big pot of vegetable soup to keep her warm.

As she poured the scalding water into her tea leaf filled cup, someone knocked on the door. It was Sherry looking worse for wear. Her skin was pale, pasty and beads of sweat formed on her brow.

Sherry handed Laurel the folded newspaper. "I thought you might want a paper." She offered.

"Thank you. Would you like to come in for a cup of tea?"

Sherry stood on the outside, looking in and then nodded and stepped onto the threshold. Laurel closed the door behind her. She gestured towards the kitchen. Laurel pulled out a chair and Sherry thankfully sat down. She swiped the sweat from her brow with the sleeve of her pelisse.

"Are you okay?" Laurel asked, concerned.

Sherry nodded. "Must be a bug going around. I'll be fine."

"I don't suppose working at the pub all night makes you feel any better?"

"Actually, it does. I love my job. I get to meet so many interesting people."

Laurel considered Sherry's remark as she poured another cup of tea for her guest.

Sherry opened the paper and pointed to the headlines. It said there was no relief of murders in London's East End, or any clue of who the killer is. Rumors were flying now that it was Jack the Ripper returned.

"This woman," Sherry said, "Is his seventh victim. It's getting so a person is afraid to go out nights."

Laurel nodded in agreement, sitting now with her cold hands wrapped around the hot tea mug. She sipped a little. It felt so comforting going down.

"I think the killer is Mr. Branson." Sherry conspiratorially said.

"Mr. Branson?" Laurel shuddered, remembering her dream while in the tub.

Sherry nodded. "He's a bit strange, don't you think?"

"A bit." Laurel admitted.

Sherry sipped her tea and put down the mug. "Well, I must be going. I need to rest up for work tonight. Thank you for the tea."

Laurel stood with Sherry and walked her to the door. "Thank you for the paper."

Sherry smiled and hurried up the stairs to her room.

Laurel returned to the kitchen, sat down and opened the paper, looking for a new flat far from Draegon Branson.

*   *   *

Laurel sat at the kitchen table writing as the vegetable soup cooked. It had been a peaceful day considering the morning's conversation with Sherry about Draegon.

She'd been preoccupied with her story when a voice came sharply into her head. "Laurel."

She shook her head thinking she imagined it when the baritone voice spoke again in a more demanding tone. "Laurel."

Laurel lowered the quill and stared into the void.

"Come Laurel. Come to me now."

Putting down the quill she stood. In a trance she turned off the stove, turned and went to the door.

Draegon opened the front door. "Laurel, what a pleasant surprise." He greeted.

"What do you want?"

"What do I want? You're the one standing at my front door." He took her hand, "Do come in."

"I can't stay long, I . . ." Draegon stopped her with a fiery kiss that melted Laurel in his arms. He swept her into his arms and carried her upstairs.

Her lips burned from his punishing kisses but she didn't care. She needed more of him; more of his icy touch against her flaming skin. Draegon more than complied with her desires. Her head tilted back, her eyes rolled and she moaned loudly as his fingers played her nubbin and nib like fine instruments.

He put his lips to her ear. "You are mine, Laurel. Do you understand? Mine and mine alone. No other man will satisfy you."

"Yours." She repeated in a heavy voice, thick with passion.

He then lifted himself atop of her and slipped his engorged phallus inside of her. They moved together in perfect harmony until at her peak of release Draegon sunk his fangs into the pulsing vein of her soft neck. Laurel cried out in ecstasy and passed out in his arms. He kissed her still lips and lay beside her, holding her close.

Chapter Eleven

*H*e heard him coming up the basement stairs. Robert waited for him in the parlor with Draegon's drink. His thoughts were on the stake in the basement. One thrust and it would be all over. He'd be free of his prison. For the past three years Robert slaved for Draegon Branson and he was tired of it. Just one thrust and life would go back to normal.

Draegon came through the dining room where Robert stood in the parlor holding his drink. The master took it from his servant and took a long drink. He peered at the young man whose heart was racing. "It wouldn't work, Robert. A stake can only paralyze a vampire not kill him." What he didn't tell him was if paralyzed Draegon couldn't remove the stake from his heart and Robert could chain him in his coffin; waiting another two hundred years before someone let him out.

Robert hated that Draegon could read his mind. He was probably reading his thoughts while he came up the stairs. How could he possibly kill the bastard if he knew what he was thinking?

"What are your plans tonight?" Draegon asked his servant.

Robert shrugged. "Just go by the pub; maybe walk around."

Draegon wickedly grinned, "Aren't you afraid of being attacked by the London serial killer?"

"I already was and I may as well be dead. It would be preferable to living this way."

Draegon feigned being hurt. "Don't you like my company? Don't I treat you right?"

Robert rolled his crystalline blue eyes and turned away from Branson. "Good night." He mumbled and grabbing his coat and hat went out the door.

Draegon laughed after him.

*   *   *

Laurel answered the knock on her apartment door but no one was there. She shook her head, wondering if she was hearing things. She turned and screamed at Draegon's unexpected appearance. "How did you get past me?" she panted, hand to heart.

Draegon shrugged.

"Well, what is it you want?" she demanded.

His molten brown eyes raked her body. Her night dress clung to her curves. Images of their love making flashed through his thoughts. He cleared his voice. "I wanted to see what you've written in my book."

"I told you, I wasn't going to write it."

"I will pay you handsomely."

"I'm sure you will, Mr. Branson."

His black eyebrows cocked. "*Mr. Branson?* Come now, don't you think we're past formalities? I mean, we were intimate."

Her face flushed. "I'd rather forget that night." If she only knew how many times he'd taken her in his arms. It made Draegon inwardly laugh. "Now, if you'll please leave." She opened the apartment door.

"Aren't you being rather rude, not offering your guest refreshment?"

"I don't consider you my guest. You're my landlord and you shouldn't be making friends with your tenants."

"Come, Laurel, I'm not above myself. I don't consider you my tenant; but . . ." he narrowed his eyes. "If you refuse to write my book and continue on this path of pretentiousness when it comes to us, I could have you put on the street."

Laurel's face turned red with anger but her stomach knotted. Would he truly put her on the street? Is that what happened to the last tenant whom Sherry claimed just disappeared one day? She also started thinking of how Sherry suspected Draegon Branson to be the serial killer. She lifted amber eyes on him. "I really think you should go now. I'll reconsider doing your book. Now if you don't mind, I'd like to go to sleep. I haven't felt well all day."

He bowed to her, "As you wish, my beloved."

"I'm not your beloved. As I said, I'm your tenant *only*: a tenant who made a big mistake by allowing you to seduce me."

His dark eyes peered at her, "You didn't stop me. Are you saying you didn't enjoy it?"

Her face reddened with shame and embarrassment. Must he torture her? "If you will please egress." She warily sighed, holding open the door.

"Very well, good night, Laurel."

"Good night, Mr. Branson."

He turned in the doorway, "I insist you call me Draegon." He said it more as a command than a suggestion.

"Fine, good night *Draegon.*"

Draegon bowed and Laurel watched him go down the steps and then heard the front door open and close. She sighed with relief and closed the door.

*   *   *

He entered his favorite pub, sat in his favorite chair and ordered his usual pint. Robert longingly looked over a few guys in the place wishing he could make a move on one of them but he was afraid Draegon would find out and kill the young man.

Draegon walked into the pub making instant eye contact with Robert. The latter gulped down a few mouthfuls of ale, trying to ignore him. By the time he put down the pint Draegon was seated across from him at the table.

"Alone tonight, Robert?"

"I'm no longer giving you men to kill. Go find your own prostitutes."

"They taste bitter and I take them as last resort to appease my hunger. Now that fellow in the brown suit, standing at the counter; his blood is sweet; I can smell it, hear it pumping through his veins." He stood and approached the man at the bar.

Robert couldn't bear to watch Draegon kill another innocent. He downed the remainder of his ale, left the money on the table and weaved between tables out the door.

*　　*　　*

As Robert drove up to the house in his phaeton he saw Laurel standing on the front step. Hearing the horses Laurel turned. Robert hopped down and approached Laurel.

"Can I help you, Miss Tuttle?"

"Is Mr. Branson at home?"

"He's out for the night."

"Oh." Laurel tapped the top of the envelope to her lips and then asked, "Can you give this to Mr. Branson? It's the first three chapters of his book."

Robert nodded and accepted the packet. He then took out the key and unlocked the front door. "Good night, Miss Tuttle."

"Good night, Mr. Hayes."

* * *

Laurel was sound asleep on the sofa. She didn't see the green fog that slithered under her apartment door. He stood over the couch, looking at her; watching her breasts move up and down with every breath. There was a hitch in his breath. She was so beautiful.

"Laurel." He whispered her name.

She opened her eyes and gasped at the sight of Draegon in her flat. "Draegon."

He took her hand, gesturing for her to stand. When she did he said, "Now take off your nightgown."

She did as he asked, dropping it on the floor. She didn't feel shy or intimidated by her nudity under his piercing stare. He reached out and undid the braid hanging over her shoulder and let the chestnut hair cascade over her shoulders, covering her breasts but her buds peeked through the veil of red. He took her in his arms and kissed her. Laurel wrapped her arms around his neck. Draegon stepped back and swiftly removed his clothing. His arousal was large and pulsing. He sat on the sofa and taking Laurel's hands encouraged her to kneel between his legs. She lifted curious eyes. Draegon gently wrapped his hand around the back of her head and pushed it down. The tip of his penis touched her lips.

"Taste me, Laurel." He passionately whispered.

Laurel moved her lips over his engorged shaft and started to suckle on it. Draegon's head fell back on the sofa as he weaved his fingers in her hair. When he felt himself ready to explode he pulled her off of him. "Lie down." He told her.

Laurel lay down and took him in her arms. His lips pressed hard against hers, tasting himself on her lips. His searing kisses nipped her bottom lip, driving him into a frenzy when he tasted her blood. He wanted Laurel more than anything in his life. His fingers stroked her nubbin. She was hot, moist and throbbing for him. He pushed his shaft into her sheath. Both moaned in pleasure. His cold body felt good against her hot skin. She bit into his shoulder as she dug her long nails into his back, drawing blood.

He couldn't wait any longer and he released himself while his fangs sunk into her neck and suckled her blood.

"Draegon. Oh, Draegon." She cried and passed out.

Draegon lifted his head and stroked her flushed cheek. "Sleep well, my beauty. In the morning this will have been a dream." He kissed her gently on her partially opened lips, stood up and dressed, wrapped the blanket around her naked body and left the same way he came in; as a green fog.

Chapter Twelve

Laurel didn't understand why she woke up naked under the blanket . . . again! What was happening to her? She felt weak and disoriented. She needed to wait a moment before she sat up and swung her feet on the hardwood floor. Laurel buried her face in her hands, upset and confused. After a few moments of gathering her thoughts she slowly stood. Laurel grabbed the arm of the sofa to steady herself in the swaying room. She took her clothes from the armoire and washed and dressed. Doing so, made her feel better. She went in the kitchen, made the coffee and ate a piece of crusty bread with jam and butter. Laurel glanced at the desk; at her latest manuscript. She finished it last evening before going to bed. It was ready to go to the papers.

*   *   *

As Laurel was coming out of her flat, Sherry was coming up the steps. She didn't look well at all. Her face was deathly white, her eyes sunken and cheeks were gaunt. "Sherry, what's wrong? Are you okay?"

She absently stared at Laurel. She pressed a smile that looked so sinister it repelled Laurel. "I'm fine. I just need sleep after working all night."

"Well, let me know if you need anything."

She only nodded and went up the steps to her apartment. Laurel saw the shadow of the door close. Shaking her head, she clung to her manuscript and exited the building.

*   *   *

Laurel saw Robert climb on the phaeton. She waved and called out to him. "Mr. Hayes?"

He turned his head. "I'll collect the rent tomorrow." He called.

Laurel caught up to where the phaeton was parked. "I was wondering if you could drive me to Oxford Street on the West End."

West End! Why didn't he think of it? He could prowl the bars around Oxford; Draegon won't find him there. At least not right away. He bobbed his head and climbed down to assist her into the phaeton.

"Thank you, Mr. Hayes, I do appreciate this."

He only nodded and closed the door. Laurel felt him climb back onto the driver's seat, the click of the rains, the horses whinny and the clip-clop of their hooves on the cobbled street as they trotted into the flow of traffic.

They shortly arrived at Oxford Street and Robert helped Laurel step down on the pavement. "What time would you like me to pick you up?" Robert asked as he climbed back into the driver's seat, taking the reins.

"I'll find a cabbie home. Thank you for taking me here."

He nodded, clicked the reins and drove away. Laurel turned with a sigh and clutching her manuscript, went off to the London Times to publish her story and receive her stipend.

*   *   *

Once home Laurel turned on the burner under the coffee pot to reheat the morning's coffee. She removed her pelisse and gloves and sat down to read the copy of the day's paper. The headlines were about the killing of a young man in the alley behind a pub. His throat was torn but very little blood was found at the scene. This led to the detectives believing the body was killed elsewhere and dumped in the alley. Even though the throat looked as if torn by some wild animal the authorities knew it was a two legged animal killing these people. There were still no clues as to a suspect.

What kind of man can tear open one's throat? Laurel wondered. It was getting more frightening that such a killer could be wandering the streets of London at nights.

Laurel turned the pages until she arrived at the section with her last story and read it with a modicum of pride.

Even while reading, Laurel worried after Sherry. She looked so peaked earlier. She hoped the girl was okay.

*   *   *

Robert parked his phaeton and started up the street on foot to find a pub. He found one, not as run down as the one he frequented in the East End but one that was quaint with men from the upper crust. He ordered a pint at the bar and glanced around at a few of the men. One in particular caught his eye. He heard the thud of the stein being put on the counter. He paid the bartender, a strapping man with dark hair and shrewd eyes, picked up his pint and weaved through a few tables until he found a small table in the back of the bar where he could observe without being too noticed.

The young man he'd been looking at turned and made eye contact. He lifted his mug in a toast to Robert. Robert smiled and returned the gesture. His heart skipped a beat as the young man approached him. He put the pint down as he pulled out a chair and sat down. He was very tall and lean with brown hair and soulful brown eyes that crinkled in the corners when he smiled. Oh yes, Robert could definitely fall in love with him. He'd never forget Brad but he wanted to move on. He wanted some happiness in his life.

The man introduced himself as Alan and Robert exchanged his name.

"So what brings you to these parts of town?"

"What makes you think I don't live in this part of town?"

"Your accent is cruder. Not that it's a bad thing; it's just how I know."

Robert smiled.

"You have a beautiful smile." Alan complimented.

"Thank you. Same to you."

And so the small talk went on as the two men got to know each other; with Robert hoping Draegon would never find out.

*   *   *

Laurel knew somehow that Draegon was at the door before she opened it. "Are you here about the first three chapters I sent over?"

He held up the packet.

"Did you put any corrections on it?"

"I did."

"Then, good night, Mr. Branson." She was about to close the door but he stopped it with his hand. "I wish to discuss it with you."

"I told you, you shouldn't keep coming here. What will people think?"

"I am your landlord, collecting rent. What people think, I don't care. Now let me in."

Against her better judgment, Laurel stepped back to let him in. He entered and she closed the door behind him.

"Shall we sit down? I would like a cup of tea."

She put the kettle of water on the stove to boil and sat across from Draegon at the small, square table.

He pushed his chair next to hers. His bergamot cologne assailed her senses. His nearness made her quiver for him; to have him take her in his arms. Her face flushed thinking about it.

"Laurel?"

She blinked her eyes, pulling herself out of her daydream. "Yes?"

"Are you okay?"

"Yes, yes. I felt a little dizzy for the moment."

He studied her. "You do look a bit pale."

"No, I'm fine. Let's get back to the story." She dismissed her thoughts.

Draegon nodded, a sly smirk on his face, for he was able to read her thoughts.

Chapter Thirteen

*L*aurel answered the door; Robert was on the other side. He seemed twitchier than normal. "I'm here for the rent." He stated. As Laurel went to retrieve the money Robert's eyes darted nervously to Sherry's door. He shifted back to Laurel as she stood before him and handed over the rent.

"Did you happen to see Miss Alocotte? Or hear her come in this morning?"

Laurel shook her head. "No, I'm just rising myself. She's probably just sound asleep." She offered the explanation.

His eyes darted to Sherry's closed door. "I'll come back later then. If she doesn't answer, I'll have to use my key." He said this more to himself than Laurel.

He tipped his hat, turned and departed. Laurel shrugged and closed the door.

Robert took a cabbie into the West End, Oxford Square to meet his friend Alan at the pub. They had a few drinks and walked along the square shopping. Afterwards, Alan invited Robert to his apartment for the most exciting sex in Robert's life. He thought Brad was great but Alan succeeded him. Alan knew how to please a man. Robert almost felt like a virgin under Alan's sexual ministrations. When finished, they lay in one another's arms and slept in the afterglow.

*   *   *

Laurel was at the desk writing when she heard the footsteps on the stairs. She assumed Robert returned for Sherry's rent. It wasn't long after she heard him run down the steps and slam the main door. She got up to peak out the door. She looked up and saw Sherry's door partially opened. Curious, she went upstairs and knocked.

"Sherry?"

No answer. After a few more soft knocks, Laurel pushed open the door and gasped. Sherry was sprawled on the floor, her face ashen, her lips blue. She stooped down beside her and deeply sighed. Before she had the chance to think, footsteps pounded up the wooden stairs and detectives burst into the loft. They momentarily stared at Laurel stooped by the body. Laurel slowly straightened and stepped back as the coroners checked the body. Sadly, they put Sherry on the stretcher and covered her with a blanket, covering her once pretty face.

"Who are you?" one of the policemen asked.

"Laurel. I live downstairs." She informed. "This is awful. Do you think the serial killer got her?"

"Hard to tell. Let's go downstairs, Miss?"

"Tuttle." She replied.

"Miss Tuttle, let's go downstairs. We have a few questions for you."

"All right." She hesitated and went down stairs.

They stood outside her door.

"When was the last time you saw the deceased?"

"About a week ago. We had tea."

"Did you do that often?"

"No, we barely spoke to each other. She was a bit odd."

"In what way was she odd?"

Beads of sweat broke out on Laurel's brow. She didn't like being cornered with these questions.

"In that she kept to herself." Robert spoke as he joined them on the stairs.

Laurel glanced at Robert and nodded to the policemen.

"Are you the landlord?"

"I'm his assistant Robert Hayes. I'm the one that brought you out here."

"Where's your landlord now?"

"Working. He should be home soon."

The policeman peered at Laurel. "Do you know if Miss Allocote had any sort of relationship with the landlord?"

"Well, I did see them together a few times." She warily reported feeling as though she was betraying the deceased.

"Together, how?" the policeman brusquely demanded.

"They were, uh . . ." she nervously glanced at Robert and then the policeman. "Caressing in the back yard."

The policeman's hand was flying over his note pad as he wrote everything down in pencil. He looked down his nose at Laurel. "And you?"

"I, uh," her face stained pink from embarrassment thinking of the relationship they had: two naked forms making love on the sofa.

"Got it." The policeman judgmentally replied, writing it down.

The other policeman looked at Robert who was staring at Laurel. "And, what about you?" the officer's voice broke into his thoughts.

Robert lifted his gaze on the officer. "I was just his assistant."

"Did you know about his relationships with the ladies?"

"Uh, no." Robert lied. "You're not thinking of accusing my master of killing Miss Allocote?" he feigned anger.

"We'd like to talk to him. In the meantime, Miss Tuttle, why don't you come with us down to the station; we'd like to ask you more questions." He took a firm grasp on her arm and led her down the steps.

Robert watched in disbelief. They were considering Miss Tuttle as a suspect.

*   *   *

"Where have you been, Robert?" Draegon's baritone voice split the darkness.

Robert jumped, startled, and rounded on his master, seated in his favorite armchair holding a glass of bourbon. "I was out. Have you no sense of what happened?"

Draegon narrowed his eyes. "I remind you who you're talking to."

"Sherry was found dead in her apartment."

"Who found her?"

"I did." He haughtily returned.

Draegon took a sip of his whiskey. "Then you know who killed her." He casually replied.

"You don't sense what happened to Miss Tuttle?"

Draegon lowered the glass from his lips. "Tell me, Robert." He seethed; his anger directed toward anyone who might have hurt her.

"The police suspect she's the killer. They have her at the police station."

Draegon crushed the glass in his hand; blood oozed over his fingers but he hardly noticed. "Were you there when they took her?"

Robert nervously nodded.

His master slowly stood; a murderous gleam in his dark eyes. "Did you try and defend her?"

"Yes." His voice squeaked as Draegon drew near.

"Not hard enough."

"I couldn't control what the police did. They learned that you had a relationship with both ladies and they assumed Miss Tuttle killed Miss Allocote in a fit of jealousy."

Draegon's hand slipped around Robert's throat. Beads of sweat broke out on his forehead. "And how did they learn this?" Draegon became more menacing.

"Miss Tuttle told them she saw you caressing Miss Langley in the back yard and inadvertently hinted that she was intimate with you."

Draegon's hand squeezed Robert's throat for what seemed a long moment as the thought of Laurel in jail raced through his mind. He let loose of Robert. The young man stumbled backwards, holding onto his bruised throat.

The enraged vampire charged out of the house to save Laurel.

*   *   *

He stood over her while she slept on the jail bunk. "Laurel." He softly commanded. "Laurel, wake up."

Her eyes fluttered open and for a moment when she saw him, thought she was dreaming. Realizing she wasn't, she swiftly sat up. "What are you doing here? How did you get in here?"

"How I got here is irrelevant. I've come to get you out of here."

"Are you insane? *You're* the reason I'm in here." She angrily hissed.

He grabbed her hand, pulling her to her feet. "I haven't time for this nonsense." He swept her into his arms.

She began kicking. "Put me down or I'll scream." She warned.

With a deep sigh he put her down but before she had the chance to triumphantly sit down, he placed a hand on her eyes. "Sleep." Laurel fell limp in his arms. He picked her up again and kicked open the cell door. Having put all of the officers in the front office in a trance when he first arrived, he carried Laurel out the front door.

Chapter Fourteen

$\mathcal{L}$aurel woke disoriented and in a strange room. She slowly sat up and waited for the dizziness to stop. She heard something at the door. Someone slipped a tray of food under the door. Laurel got up and hurried to the door: a door with bars on the top half.

She gripped the bars and pulled herself up on her toes. "Hello?"

Robert's face appeared.

"Mr. Hayes, where am I? Why are you sliding food under the door?"

"You're in Mr. Branson's house on the third floor. He fixed the room to your comfort."

"Why? Why did he put me in here?"

"For your protection." Robert partially lied. Draegon had every intention of making her his bride.

"He took me from one prison to another. Tell him I want to see him; immediately." She commanded.

"He'll come later." Hayes assured, turned and walked away; hearing Laurel rattle the bars, hollering.

Frustrated, Laurel took her tray and put it on the small, round table. She pulled up a chair and removed the lids over the dishes. The aroma of the baked chicken made her stomach growl. She was starving. She hadn't eaten in a while. Laurel was confused by what day it was and how long she'd been in this room. She drank the wine. It was sweet with a metallic taste. Laurel was thirsty so she gulped it down like water. By the time she finished eating and drinking, Laurel's body felt heavy. Her eyes could barely stay open so she climbed into bed, pulling the covers up to her chin. She fell asleep as soon as her head hit the pillow.

*   *   *

The door creaked open and softly closed. Draegon approached the bed and smiled down at Laurel; innocently sleeping. He almost hated to wake her up but his need to have her overwhelmed him. He divested his clothes and climbed in the bed beside her. He stroked her cheek. "Laurel." His voice drifted into her dreams. "Laurel, wake up."

Her eyes fluttered open and stared into the dark, sinister but sensual eyes. His lips came down hard and determined. Laurel moaned beneath him.

His hand moved up her smooth stomach to her breast. He rubbed the hardened nipple with the palm of his thumb. Laurel's breathing grew rapid. She started to undulate beneath his hip and leg wrapped around her. Her arms clung to his neck, her head tossed back. The pulsing vein was calling to him. Draegon kept control. His hand slid down her thigh until his fingers found the soft bush on the moist lips. He expertly stroked the nubbin. Laurel squealed beneath him. His fingers delved deeper into the chasm. He watched Laurel squeal and squirm, clinging desperately to his neck. She bit his shoulder. Draegon's control was waning. He couldn't wait any further to claim her. He thrust his sword into her sheath. Laurel cried out as he took her. Together they rode the tide of passion until just before their climax, Draegon sunk his fangs into her soft neck and suckled her sweet blood. Laurel screamed in fiery delight as he continued his thrusting until they exploded.

Draegon lay atop of Laurel while she gasped for air. He ran his hand over her damp, chestnut hair that shimmered red in the candlelight. She was so beautiful and she was *his*.

"Draegon?"

"Yes, my beloved?"

"Is this a dream?"

Her question surprised him. "No."

"I shouldn't have done this. *You shouldn't have done this to me. I feel enough shame.*"

"For all of your prudish ways, you enjoyed having sex?" he almost laughed.

Laurel flushed. "Why am I here in this room?"

"To protect you from the police. You did escape jail after all."

Her green eyes burned him. She angrily pushed him off of her and sat up. "*You're* the one who took me out of jail."

81

"Is that where you'd rather be right now?"

She averted her eyes. "No." She flashed her gaze on him. "But you took me from one prison to another."

"Darling, you're not my prisoner," he lied. "But the detectives are watching this building and I can't take the chance they'll see you pass a window."

"How long will I have to be here?" she lamented.

"Just until they realize you didn't kill Miss Allocote."

He pressed her back into the pillows. "Rest now. Robert will bring you breakfast in the morning." He lay his hand over her eyes. "Sleep, my beloved."

Her eyes fluttered close and her breathing grew shallow. He stroked her warm cheek, stood, dressed and quit the room.

* * *

"What's wrong?"

Robert deeply sighed as the two men walked into Alan's flat. "Nothing, why do you ask?" He removed his hat and jacket.

Alan tossed his own hat on the bed. "You've been quiet most of the evening. Didn't you like the restaurant I took you to?"

Robert pressed a smile. "The restaurant and food were fine."

"Then, what's wrong? Did I say or do something wrong?"

*It's what **I** did that's wrong.* Robert thought: *Leaving that poor girl in the devious hands of his master Draegon. How could he be such a horrible cad?* Robert believed he could have a decent relationship with another but it was all based on a lie. How did he tell Alan that he was the lackey for a monster? That it's his master killing all of those innocent people; his beloved Brad included.

Alan started to unbutton Robert's shirt. "You can tell me anything, you know that."

No, I can't! Robert silently lamented. He stopped Alan's fingers from moving down his chest. Alan looked inquisitively at Robert.

"I'm sorry, Alan, I can't do this tonight—or any night." Robert stammered. He deftly buttoned his shirt. He reached for his jacket and picked up his hat. "I must leave."

Alan stood dumbfounded and hurt. "Robert, why? We don't have to have sex, we can just sit and talk if you'd like."

Robert shook his tousled blonde hair going for the door. "No. I'm sorry, Alan, I thought I could have a serious relationship but I can't. Bye." He choked, dashed out the door, and down the hall.

Alan heard his footsteps heavy on the stairs. He spun about and sat on the bed. He covered his face in his hands and cried.

*   *   *

Robert quietly entered the house, hoping Draegon was out. He jumped when the lamp went on in the parlor. He faced his master, seated in his favorite chair with a glass of bourbon in his hand.

"Where have you been, Robert?" his dark voice demanded.

"Out."

"Where? You weren't at your favorite watering hole. Have you been keeping secrets from me, Robert?"

"No, just keeping my business to myself." He retorted and started for the stairs to avoid the confrontation.

"You have a new lover." Draegon accused; he cursed himself that Laurel's distraction kept him from being sharper towards Robert.

Robert paused. Hand rested on the banister he looked at Draegon. "Okay, I *did* have a new lover but it's over. I ended it tonight. I couldn't risk the chance you would find him and kill him. In fact, I realized tonight I can't have *any* relationship because of you." He barked and hurried up the stairs.

Draegon wickedly laughed. "And that's the way it's supposed to be, Robert. You are my slave. You live for my commands." He chuckled again, lifting the glass of bourbon to his lips.

Chapter Fifteen

Laurel emerged from the bathroom drying her hair after a hot bath. She changed into a clean night rail—since that was the only clothing Draegon left her—and sat before the roaring fire in the hearth to beat the chill and hasten the drying of her hair. She combed out the long chestnut hair, that sparkled like bright copper, wondering what she had done to deserve this imprisonment.

Something slid under the door. It was a packet of papers. Laurel rushed to the bars at the door, standing on her tip-toes. "Mr. Hayes?" she desperately called. "Mr. Hayes?"

He glanced up at her peering eyes and fingers gripping the bars. "Please let me out."

"I'm sorry; you'll need to ask Mr. Branson." He mechanically replied and walked away.

Laurel continued to cling to the bars long after he walked away. Ruefully, she returned to the stool before the fire to continue combing out her hair.

She remembered, all too clearly, the incident from last evening; when she foolishly gave herself to Draegon. Her face flushed thinking about it. "What is wrong with me?" she lamented. "What kind of woman have I become?" Not one who would marry into a decent family now. She ruined her reputation with Mr. Branson. She covered her face with her hands and started to cry.

Laurel spied the packet on the floor that Mr. Hayes put there. She dashed the tears from her eyes and moved to pick it up. She untied the folder and looked inside. They were the notes and first three chapters she had written of Mr. Branson's book. She angrily threw it on the floor; papers scattered over the old wood flooring. She anxiously looked around the room; but for the clock on the mantel, Laurel would not know the time of day it was as there was no window in the room. She feared she'd go insane if she had to stay in here much longer. Laurel threw herself on the bed and clutched the pillow. Her life as she'd known it; was over.

*   *   *

"Good evening, my sweet; I trust you enjoyed dinner?"

Laurel lifted raging eyes on Draegon standing beside her.

"It was passable." She snipped, dabbing her mouth. It was actually delicious but she wouldn't give him the satisfaction.

"Too bad; Robert will be sorry to hear it."

She wanted to retract her words but thought better of it. "What do you want?" she sneered.

"Must we play this game, Laurel?"

"It's *you* playing a game; keeping me here, having your way with me whenever you want."

"Having my way with you? You give yourself so willingly."

Her face reddened. "Only because you catch me at vulnerable moments."

"You could stop me."

"Hmmph, as if I could. You're quite persistent."

"And you enjoy every minute of it." He retorted.

"Well, you won't have your way with me anymore." She snipped.

He snatched her wrist, leaning down into her face. "I will not have you dictate to me when I can have you."

"I'd rather be in jail then." She muttered.

"You'd be hung for Miss Allocote's murder."

"But I didn't kill her." She retorted.

"I know you didn't."

She narrowed green eyes at him. "How could you be so sure?"

He wickedly grinned. "I know you, my darling. Now," he took her hand. Laurel automatically stood, staring into his molten chocolate eyes. "Let's not talk any more of prisons."

Her face reddened and she fumbled a step. "If I'm not a prisoner . . ."

He put a finger on her trembling lips. "Shh, shh!"

"I could be here forever." She lamented. Draegon sat her on the side of the bed.

He subtly smiled. *Yes, that's my intention! For us to be together forever!*

She turned aside from him, blinking back the tears. He heard her sniffle and sat beside her. He poked a finger in her right cheek, turning her head to face him. Lust burned in his eyes. He smelled the sweetness of her blood, heard it pumping through her veins; to the main one pulsing in her neck. The beaded nipples pressed against the gauze of the nightgown. It took all of his control not to throw her back on the bed and ravish her. "Do not cry, my darling Laurel, it will all be okay." He assured in a whisper. He folded her into his arms and let her cry into his shirt.

Laurel pulled away, dashing her tears, embarrassed by her weak emotions. "I can't live like this. There's not even a window I can look out of."

"For now, it has to be. I sent up the notes and chapters of my story. With nothing to distract you, you can finish it and I'll be here to help in any way I can."

He noted the packet of papers on the desk. "You'll feel better when you get back to doing what you like most; writing."

Laurel looked down at her folded hands.

Draegon deeply sighed. "Very well, I'll leave you to your work. I must go out. I will check in on you later."

She didn't answer and Draegon quit the room.

* * *

Robert sat in his usual booth, at his usual watering hole, sipping ale. He missed Sherry's presence. And he hated himself for allowing that monster to get away with murder. Now he was about to turn a lovely, innocent young woman into the same creature as himself. His eyes darted about the room, looking for a prospect for the night. He would resort to the alley again, for that was the only kind of relationship he could risk. He swore to himself that he would never get involved with another partner; not while Draegon existed.

He noticed a young man eyeing him from the bar. Robert raised his mug to the man and he sauntered over to Robert's booth. He slid in across from him. "'Evenin', mate." He greeted Robert.

"'Evenin'." Robert returned the greeting.

The man extended his hand, "Paul's the name."

"Robert. Can I buy you a drink?"

"Ale would be fine." Paul replied.

Robert waved down a barmaid and she took the order, walking away.

"I've seen you here a few times before." Paul commented, his brown eyes roaming over Robert's buffed physique well-fitted in a suit of dark blue. "You're quite the generous lover."

Robert's face flushed as he sipped the ale. "I've had many friends over the years."

The barmaid returned with Paul's pint and went back to the bar to fill more orders from other customers.

Paul leaned to Robert and said in a low voice; though he doubted anyone would be listening, considering the bawdy crowd. "I hope I can be added to that list."

Robert smiled. "We'll see what the night brings."

*   *   *

Robert and Paul were pressed against the wall of the alleyway, bruising one another's lips with their kisses. Before Robert got the chance to suckle Paul's nipples, he was flung aside. He hit the opposite wall and bounced on the ground. He watched in disgust as Draegon made a meal of Paul's blood. He got up and started to slip away. Draegon turned, swiping the back of his hand over his bloody lips and licked his fangs of the metallic red liquid before retracting them.

"Robert."

The young man stopped and slowly faced his master in the darkness of the alley way.

"I want you to go home and look after our guest."

Robert nodded, turned, and quietly walked away.

Chapter Sixteen

*R*obert peeked through the bars before setting down the tray of food. Laurel was fervently writing at the table. He felt awful; her being a prisoner. He understood, well, what it was like. Although he wasn't locked away in a room, Robert lived in his own personal hell, being slave to Draegon Branson. He set down the tray, pulled the small metal object from his dove gray jacket and turned the key before sliding the food under the door.

Laurel lifted her intense gaze from the words on the paper when she heard the slide of the tray on the wooden floor and the click of the key in the lock. She set down the quill and went to the door. She grabbed the bars, pulling herself up, and searched the dark area beyond for Robert but he was gone. Gripping the doorknob, she slowly turned it. It clicked open. She pushed the tray aside with her bare foot and pulled the heavy door open. Laurel peeked out. She carefully crept out of the room and stood in the dark hallway. Looking up and down, Laurel made the decision to go right.

Sliding her hand along the dusty wall for support, Laurel wound up in a large, master suite its décor of the early 1700's. The drapes were so dusty and thread worn they would fall apart at the touch of a hand. Over the large, four-poster bed was a large oil portrait of a young woman dressed in clothes from the eighteenth century and, at closer inspection Laurel found an uncanny resemblance to herself.

She fumbled around the musty room. She opened the bed stand drawer. Lying in the drawer was a small journal. Laurel reached for it until a deep voice boomed.

"What are you doing in here?"

Laurel swiftly removed her hand and shut the drawer with her knee. She turned at the waist. "Is that your fiancée?"

"Was."

"She was very pretty."

"I know. Now, go back to your room. I will deal with Mr. Hayes, severely, for letting you out of the room." He snarled.

"Did the police catch the killer?" she hopefully asked.

"Not according to the papers. Now, let's go."

She huffed and sat hard on the side of the bed; dust blew up from the covers. Draegon inwardly groaned. *Why must she be so stubborn?*

"Is this your room?"

"Yes." He partially lied. It was his room before he became a creature of the night.

"It looks like it hasn't been cleaned in a hundred years." She ran her fingers through the dust on the bed stand.

"Laurel . . ." he was beginning to lose his patience and his lustful control of her body.

She lifted woeful green eyes. He pulled her into his arms and bruised her lips with his deep, passionate kiss. Laurel moaned against him, sliding her arms around his neck. He smelled like bergamot. Laurel sniffed in his scent, never wanting to let him go or the kiss to stop. Neither did Draegon.

He pressed her down on the bed while starting to divest of his clothes. Draegon lay naked atop of her, his lips clinging once more to hers. His kiss trailed to her chin, her throat, to the soft breasts pressed against the gauzy material of her night rail. "Laurel." He huskily whispered. Draegon peeled away the top of her gown to her waist, exposing the rosy, hard nipples. He groaned as he took one in his mouth and suckled on it.

Laurel arched her back, aching for more of his touch. She felt his hardness against her thigh.

Draegon pulled off the gown, enjoying the sight of her nudity and the body that was his. His hand ran up and down her inner thigh before he slipped his fingers into the moist patch between her legs.

Laurel gasped as he stroked the walls of her sheath. "Oh, Draegon!" she cried out. She grabbed his hand, pushing his fingers in deeper and harder.

Oh, yes, she was definitely his!

When they reached their climax and Draegon partook of her sustaining blood, he held Laurel in his arms. She had passed out, as she always did when he drank her blood at the peak of coitus. He stroked her damp hair and kissed her brow. He glanced up at the picture of his fiancée. She and Laurel strongly resembled physically but the resemblance stopped there. He didn't fall in love with Lenora, his past fiancée but with Laurel; the hot blooded woman of the present. She was as strong and determined as Lenora was weak and unsure of herself. How could her reincarnation be so different?

His gaze drifted to the window. Specks of dawn were beginning to show. He needed to get Laurel back to her room and him, his coffin. Draegon quickly dressed them both and carried Laurel out of the master suite.

Draegon laid her on the bed and bent to kiss her brow. "Sleep, my darling. Soon there will be no more suffering. You will live blissfully as my bride through eternity."

*   *   *

Robert was pinned to the wall by Draegon's hand around his throat. Robert wished he would kill him. He'd had enough of being this lunatic's servant.

"You let her out?" Draegon hollered, slamming Robert hard against the wall. "I found her walking about the house in places she shouldn't be. She is there for her protection."

"You're keeping here there for your own selfish reasons."

"What I do is none of your business. You pathetic oaf." He snarled, and with one last hard slam, let Robert slump to the floor, unconscious.

*   *   *

The woman stood alone on the edge of the pier looking out over the choppy Thames. Her husband was lost at sea when his merchant ship got caught up in a storm. She deeply sighed; she missed him so much. The woman turned, thinking she heard something behind her. She couldn't peer through the darkness. As she turned back to look out over the water, something grabbed her from behind. The woman barely had the time to scream as the vampire tore into her neck with his massive fangs. Blood gurgled in her throat. Draegon tossed her into the Thames where she would meet her husband in the watery grave.

Draegon stopped in a pub, his blood lust un-satiated. As he held onto a mug of beer, he watched the local patrons. Most were drunk. They would make easy targets. He particularly watched a middle aged man seated at the bar. Draegon called over the barmaid and told her to send the man whatever he was drinking on him. When the man received the drink he turned about and holding up his pint, smiled at Draegon. He slid off of the bar stool and staggered to Draegon's table.

"Adam's the name." he introduced with a slur.

"I'm not here for chatting. I came here for one thing only. Shall we go out back?" he lured.

The man's dark eyes widened, delighted by the prospect. Taking a hearty gulp from his pint, he stood. Draegon followed. Together they casually walked out to the alley. Draegon threw him against the wall, pressing himself against him, searing the man's lips with his own. The man moaned in his mouth. He fumbled for Draegon's front flap of his pants and fished for the engorging penis. He wrapped his fingers around it and started pumping the organ. Draegon's breath grew ragged as he pushed Adam's hand away. As Adam was in the throes of climax, Draegon sunk his fangs into his neck. Adam cried out in pain and ecstasy before Draegon dropped his corpse on the ground. Swiping the blood from his mouth with the back of his hand, Draegon hurried away.

*   *   *

It was close to dawn when Draegon arrived home. He checked in on Laurel before going to his coffin. She was sound asleep. He turned the knob; it was locked. All was secure. He went downstairs.

Chapter Seventeen

She woke feeling drained of energy. As she started to sit up, the room started to spin. Laurel laid her head back on the propped pillow and waited for her world to settle down. She noticed the tray of breakfast on the floor. Laurel slowly got out of bed, holding onto the post; waited a moment and crossed to the door. She stood on tip toes to peek out of the bars. Mr. Hayes wasn't nearby. Out of curiosity, she tried the door knob but to her disappointment, it was locked. With a deep sigh she sat at the table and began to eat her breakfast. She needed to get that journal. Laurel was sure it was important to the biography. It would probably fill in a lot of the gaps.

After breakfast, with a cup of tea at hand, Laurel spread out the papers and dipped the quill in the inkpot. Perhaps when Mr. Hayes returned for the breakfast tray Laurel could convince him to either let her out or for him to go to the master suite and retrieve the book.

*   *   *

Robert watched Laurel a few moments before knocking on the door for Laurel to slip the empty tray under the door; at which point he would give her the lunch tray. She was feverishly writing: most likely Draegon's biography. What lies were in those notes? Robert was sure he made himself look the perfect, charming gentleman. He rapped his knuckles on the door and Laurel looked up with a gasp she was so intense writing.

She stood up with the empty tray and hurried to the door. She slid it under the door. Moments later she received another tray with lunch. Laurel grabbed the bars, standing on her tip-toes. "Mr. Hayes, would you please let me out for a moment. I need to retrieve a journal so that I can complete the biography for Mr. Branson."

He stared at her a moment and then turned away.

"Mr. Hayes? Mr. Hayes?"

He twisted at the waist, seeing her desperate expression. He returned to the door. "I'm sorry, I can't let you out." He said, remembering the consequences from the evening before.

"No, no, listen. Could you go the master suite and retrieve the journal for me? It's in the left bed stand drawer. I'm sure Mr. Branson would want me to have it."

Robert hesitated a moment, then nodded and walked away. Laurel was elated. She paced the room until he returned. He slipped the small book through the bars and

Laurel took it, holding it close to her bosom. "Thank you, Mr. Hayes."

He bobbed his head and exited the hallway.

Robert sat in the parlor reading the newspaper he acquired from someone's step. If Draegon found him reading it, he'd be livid. Fortunately, it was morning and he was in a deep slumber in his coffin. The headline announced another body washed up against the piers. The police still haven't a clue how the suspect is killing his victims.

There was nothing said about Miss Tuttle or her escape. They had to figure that she was innocent and dismissed any charges. If only he could help her escape that room, this house and that madman Draegon. Robert knew that any attempt on Laurel's part to leave would be futile. He would hunt her down until he found her. He was determined to make her his bride and to do that he would have to turn her into a vampire, like himself. He felt guilty there was nothing he could do to save her from such a horrible fate.

*   *   *

Laurel sat on the bed and began to read the journal:

I met my fiancée today. He is quite handsome: black hair to his shoulders and deep dark eyes. His physique is tall and slightly more than average built. He's very charming, yet, there's something about him I don't trust. There's an evil essence about him I can't explain.

Laurel's heart quickened. That was exactly how she felt about Draegon.

> *My instincts are warning me not to go through with the wedding. My parents won't hear of it. The merger of our two families will bring them the prestige they've been seeking. They just don't understand. Can no one else see Mr. Branson as I do?*
>
> *He's a monster! A horrible monster! I saw him attack a woman by the pier as I was strolling by it with my maid—my chaperone. Fangs descended from his mouth and I saw him penetrate the woman's neck and rip her throat. Blood spewed everywhere. I screamed. My maid jumped. She obviously didn't see it. Mr. Branson turned when he heard me scream. His eyes seemed to glow in the twilight. I saw him swipe his mouth of the blood and his fangs disappeared into his upper gums. He started toward me, looking human again, a look of remorse on his face: only that I caught him and not what he had done. I screamed again and ran; my maid quickly followed.*
>
> *"Lenora!" he shouted after me. But I kept running.*

How could I marry a monster? He frightened me before but now he terrified me. Surely my parents would agree with me now and call the authorities to take him away.

My parents claimed I was imagining things. Why would I imagine such a horrible thing? They claimed it my way to get out of the marriage; that my abigail didn't see anything, just heard me scream and then run. All she said was that Mr. Branson was walking towards us. He seemed quite upset by my reaction to the sight of him.

As I look at my reflection in the standing mirror in my wedding gown, my spirits descended. I could not go through with this! My fiancée was a monster; a murderer. I must end it all.

That was her last entry. Laurel shuddered as she closed the book. Draegon Branson is the killer of all those people found dead all about the East End for the past few months; at least that Laurel was aware of. He killed Sherry. The girl tried to warn her. Had she seen him kill anyone? Did he know it and murdered her to silence her? What did she do now?

He kept her locked away from any contact. He said it was for her protection from the police but Laurel began believing he had other plans for her. She wondered: were the authorities looking for her? He did take her from jail. As far as the police saw it, she escaped. How was she to escape this room?

Chapter Eighteen

*H*e slipped under the door in a green mist and reformed beside her bed. Tonight was the night he would turn her to his dark world. He stripped of his clothes and climbed into bed next to her. His lips trailed feathered kisses on her brow, cheeks and then covered her mouth with his. Laurel responded in her hazy state, moaning into his mouth and slipping her arms around his neck. He lowered his head to the rosy buds hard for his touch. He wrapped his lips around one breast and cupped the other, kneading the nipple. Laurel groaned, arching her back to him. His breathing grew ragged as he slid his hand down her soft abdomen to the chestnut fur between her legs. He pried the lips apart and stroked the nubbin. She was moist and ready for him.

"Wake up, my beloved." He whispered as he lifted himself to insert his shaft into her sheath.

Laurel's eyes fluttered open. Upon seeing him atop of her, she screamed and pushed at his chest to get him off of her. Draegon pinned her down.

"Laurel, it's me. It's Draegon." He consoled her.

"I know who and what you are. Get off of me, you monster."

"What do you know about me?" he sneered, his face a breath away from hers.

She defiantly glared at him, "You're the monster going around killing all of those innocent people. You killed Sherry and let me take the blame."

"I got you out of jail." He retorted. "And yes, I killed all of those people. It's what a vampire does. He doesn't kill for the fun of it; he hunts. He needs the blood of others to survive."

"That's supposed to make me feel affection for you?" she hotly returned. "I feel nothing but contempt for you. Now get off of me."

He put more pressure on her. "I will not. Tonight, I bring you to completion. When you waken, you will be my bride and we will exchange our vows and mingle our blood beneath the blood moon."

Laurel continued to struggle beneath him. Her efforts were futile. His punishing kisses seared her lips. His fingers delved deep into her, making her scream with ecstasy and anger. He lifted his head and watched the emotions flood her face. Her eyes rolled back in her head, she arched her hips, her body shamelessly demanding more of his touch. He chuckled, ramming his head into her hot, moist feminine sheath.

"Draegon!" she called out. "Oh, my Draegon!"

He pressed his lips to her neck, "You understand now. You are mine, I am yours."

As she was ready to climax, he plunged his fangs into her neck, suckling hard the remainder of her blood. When finished, he got up and dressed. He bent over her and caressed her cold cheek. "Soon, my beloved, you will rise as my bride. Nothing will stand in the way of our happiness."

*   *   *

Robert studied Laurel through the bars after sliding a meal to her. She was in an ethereal repose. He quickly unlocked the door and moved to Laurel's bedside. He touched her hand; it was ice cold and stiff. *Oh no! He did it! The bastard killed Laurel!* Perhaps there was still time to save her.

He crept down the basement. Draegon would be waking soon to suck his blood and manipulate his cock. The beast claimed the blood tasted better when his victim was in the throes of climax. He picked up the wooden 2" x 4" stake and slowly opened the coffin lid. He stared down at the vampire in his repose. He didn't have much time and he had to get it right the first time. He couldn't coward out. Robert raised the stake over his head and with one swift thrust, plunged the sharpened instrument into Draegon's chest.

The monster screamed in agony as his body became paralytic. Robert stepped away from the coffin, covering his ears. Blood had spurted onto his clothes. He felt sick. Was he as bad as the creature that killed others? But wait, if he remembered what Draegon told him the last time he tried to stake him; the stake only paralyzed him. It's how he found him that night in the cemetery. How he regretted waking him. If he locked and chained shut the lid of his coffin, Draegon Branson would remain paralyzed forever.

As he stared at the creature with blood oozing on his shirt, his eyes staring blankly at the ceiling, something shoved him aside. He fell into a stack of boxes. He stared at Laurel. Fangs formed over her lower lip, her eyes were bright green. She hissed at him and turned to remove the stake from her lover's heart.

Robert picked up another piece of thick wood hoping to swing it hard enough to break her neck. "No!" he hollered, charging her.

Laurel took hold of his wrist and twisted it. Robert felt it crack. His arm was broken. She shoved him away. Her newfound strength sent him sailing a few feet across the cellar. Laurel turned to Draegon and with one tug, removed the bloody stake. She watched as the wound began to heal. She heard Robert charging her again. She thrust out her hand and picked him up by the throat, holding him over her head. She squeezed tighter.

"Let him go." Draegon spoke behind her.

She glimpsed her lover, and then Robert. She gave him a slight toss and turned to Draegon. "Are you sure we should let him go?" she asked.

"He's just a pathetic little man. He won't say or do anything." He proffered his arm. "Come my darling, let us prepare for our wedding."

Laurel smiled and looped arms.

As the couple walked away, they heard Robert say, "I tried, Laurel. I tried to save you from this fate. I'm so sorry."

She lifted her green eyes on Draegon. "What does he mean?"

"Nothing, he's just babbling. Come."

The two climbed the cellar steps.

*   *   *

The moon was a deep red. Draegon and Laurel stood beneath the window, gazing into one another's eyes. He bit into his wrist and encouraged her to do the same. She obeyed. He pressed their wrists together as blood ran down their arms. "Tonight you are my beloved bride. I shall cherish you through all eternity. Together we will walk the dark journey ahead of us."

"Tonight you are my beloved husband. I shall cherish you through all eternity. Together we will walk the dark journey ahead of us." She added, "And I will enjoy every moment."

They embraced, their lips pressing passionately. He lifted her into his arms and tossed her on the bed. No more being gentle. Laurel was now one of his kind; her passion will be just as fierce. They hungered for blood. They sunk their fangs into one another's shoulders. Laurel raked his back, drawing blood. She licked at her fingers.

He flipped her over, stroking her lower lips and rammed his engorged penis into her dark, moist cavern. Laurel cried out with ecstasy, gripping the pillow as he rutted her from behind. He bit her neck and licked the blood trickling out. The smell of it aroused them further.

Draegon finished and knelt on the bed, turning her around. Laurel scrambled to her knees. He sliced open his chest. Blood flowed freely. Laurel growled and suckled it, growing more excited and stronger with each gulp. Draegon threw back his head and groaned. He grew weaker from her guzzling his blood. He pulled her away and kissed the blood on her lips. Draegon pressed her down again and mounted her once more. He thrust harder, harder, until Laurel started to cry out from orgasm. He plunged his fangs into her neck moments before the explosive finish. They fell into a lover's embrace.

Epilogue

Robert sat at a pub on the West side of London. He had procured a flat in the area. For the first time he felt free. Draegon and his bride moved to Romania. He felt bad that he couldn't save her from the awful fate of being a vampire but he could no longer dwell on it.

He saw a young man at the bar watching him. Robert inwardly smiled, sending a drink over. The man held up his glass in cheers. Robert did the same. The man came over to the table. "Blake." He introduced himself

Robert extended his hand for the shake. "Robert. Won't you join me?"

Blake nodded and sat at the table. Robert hadn't felt so relaxed with a man. He needn't fear Draegon killing another lover. He was free to love once more.

Ms. Markowicz is a prolific author of a variety of genres but her favorite is vampire/horror. Her interests in vampires started when, as a little girl, watched Dracula with her father. It became an ongoing thing to watch the classic horror movies at night with her dad.

Her interest remained peaked through her teen age life when Dark Shadows appeared on television. Her love for vampires only strengthened over the years and now writes her own vampire/horror novels.

She attended the Art Institute for video production and film directing.

Presently, she lives in Philadelphia with her husband, four sons and three cats.